This book belongs to

_____

_____

_____

To Gabrielle
–CL

For my two little mice
–AE

tiger tales
an imprint of ME Media, LLC
202 Old Ridgefield Road, Wilton, CT 06897
This paperback edition published in the United States 2008
Published in hardcover in the United States 2004
Originally published in Great Britain 2004
by Little Tiger Press
an imprint of Magi Publications
Text copyright ©2004 Christine Lesson
Illustrations copyright ©2004 Andy Ellis

Library of Congress Cataloging-in-Publication Data
Leeson, Christine, 1965-
 Just for you! / by Christine Leeson ; illustrated by Andy Ellis.
    p. cm.
 Summary: When the mice children accidentally break their mother's birthday present,
they venture out to find something to replace it.
  ISBN-13 978-1-58925-042-0 (hardcover)
 ISBN-10 1-58925-042-7 (hardcover)
 ISBN-13 978-1-58925-408-4 (paperback)
 ISBN-10 1-58925-408-2 (paperback)
 [1. Mothers—Fiction. 2. Birthdays—Fiction. 3. Mice—Fiction.] I. Ellis, Andy, ill. II. Title.
 PZ7.L51565Ju 2004
 [E]—dc22
                                          2004017272
                  ISBN-13: 978-1-58925-408-4
                  ISBN-10: 1-58925-408-2
                      Printed in China

JUST FOR YOU!

by Christine Leeson

Illustrated by Andy Ellis

tiger tales

Jenny opened her eyes. It was a sweet summer morning and it was so early the sun was barely up.

"Wake up," Jenny whispered to her brothers and sister. "It's Mom's birthday today. We have to wrap her present."

All the mice jumped out of bed.

"I'll help!" cried Jenny's sister excitedly.

"I'll help, too!"

"And, me!"

Jenny stepped back as the mice pushed forward. "Be careful!" she cried. "You'll break…!"

SMASH!

It was too late. The present was pulled from Jenny's paws and shattered on the ground.

"Oh no," said Jenny, looking at the broken gift. "Maybe we can find something else before Mom wakes up. Come on, everybody!"

The mice scampered outside. Overhead, the sky
was still flushed with the pink sunrise.

"This way," called Jenny, but her older brother
had already seen something in the shadows.

"Look, look!" he shouted. "How about these?"
Next to the path there was a cluster of juicy red
strawberries.

"*Mm*, what a treat!" Jenny said, licking
her lips. "Mom will love them!"

At that moment Vole scurried out of the dewy grass.

"Thank you," she said. "You've found my strawberries. I was carrying some home for my family's breakfast when I dropped a few. I've really got my paws full here!"

"Oh," said Jenny, feeling disappointed. "We thought we'd found a present for our mother."

"Maybe she'd like something
else instead," said Vole. "How
about those?" She nodded toward
some feathers caught between two
branches of a nearby bush.

"Oh yes! They'll make a lovely soft pillow!" said Jenny, and she scampered off to gather them. "Mom will be so surprised. This is going to be the best birthday present ever!"

But just then Bluejay chirped from above,
"My feathers! Thank goodness you've found
them. I need them to line my nest and keep
my eggs warm."

"You'd better take them then," said Jenny.
"They would have made a nice present for
our mother's birthday, though."

Bluejay thought for a moment. "Does your mother like flowers?" she asked. "I can see a nice one in the grass just over there."

"Oh thank you!" cried Jenny, and the mice scurried off as fast as they could.

The grass was very tall and the little
mice had to push and scramble through it
in search of the flower.

"I can't see it anywhere," cried Jenny.

"I see it!" shouted her little brother.

"Quick, Jenny! Over here!"

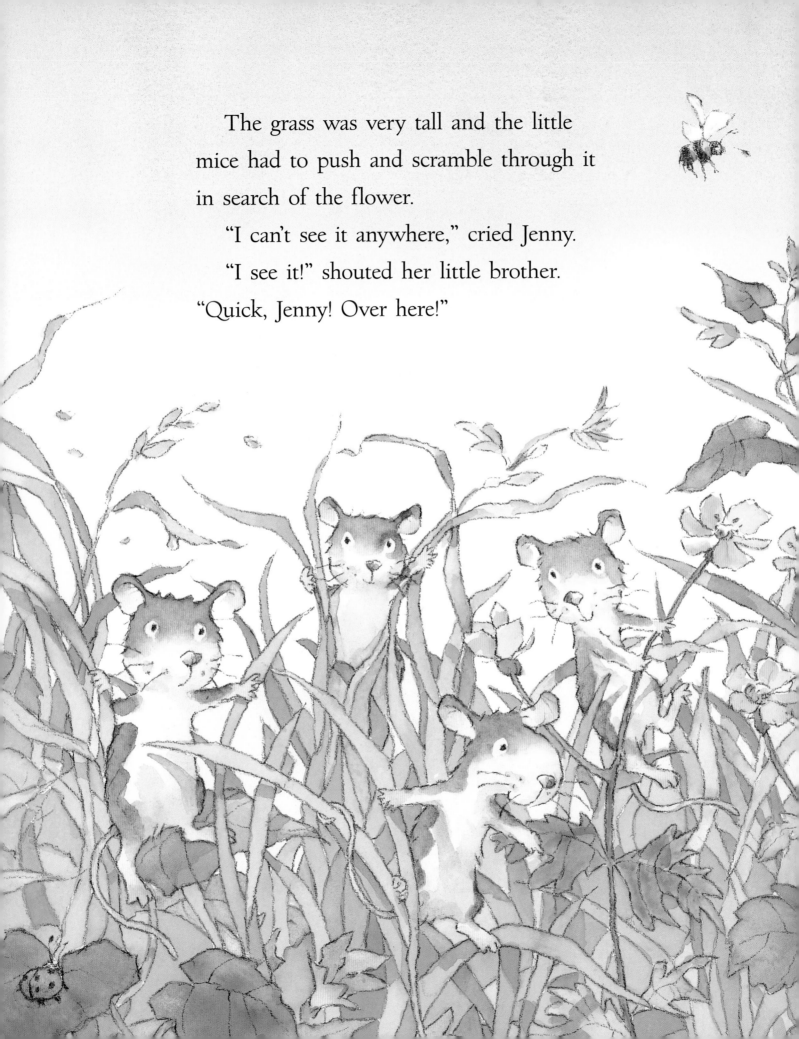

He picked up a large white daisy and waved it over his head. "Do you think Mom will like it?" he asked, stumbling under the flower's weight.

"She'll love it!" Jenny said. "It will make a beautiful present! Let's hurry back home before she wakes up."

Just then Rabbit hopped over. "Wait, wait!" he called. "That's my flower! My grandma's not feeling well and I was going to take it home for her. I put it down for a minute and then it was gone."

"Oh, we're sorry," said Jenny. "You should take it for her. We can find another present for our mother."

"Thank you, little mice," said Rabbit as he hopped away. "I hope you find something soon."

Jenny scratched her head. The sun was climbing over the trees into the deep blue sky. Their mother would be waking up soon and they still hadn't found a birthday present.

Suddenly something fluttered across the path. Jenny leaped up and grabbed it...

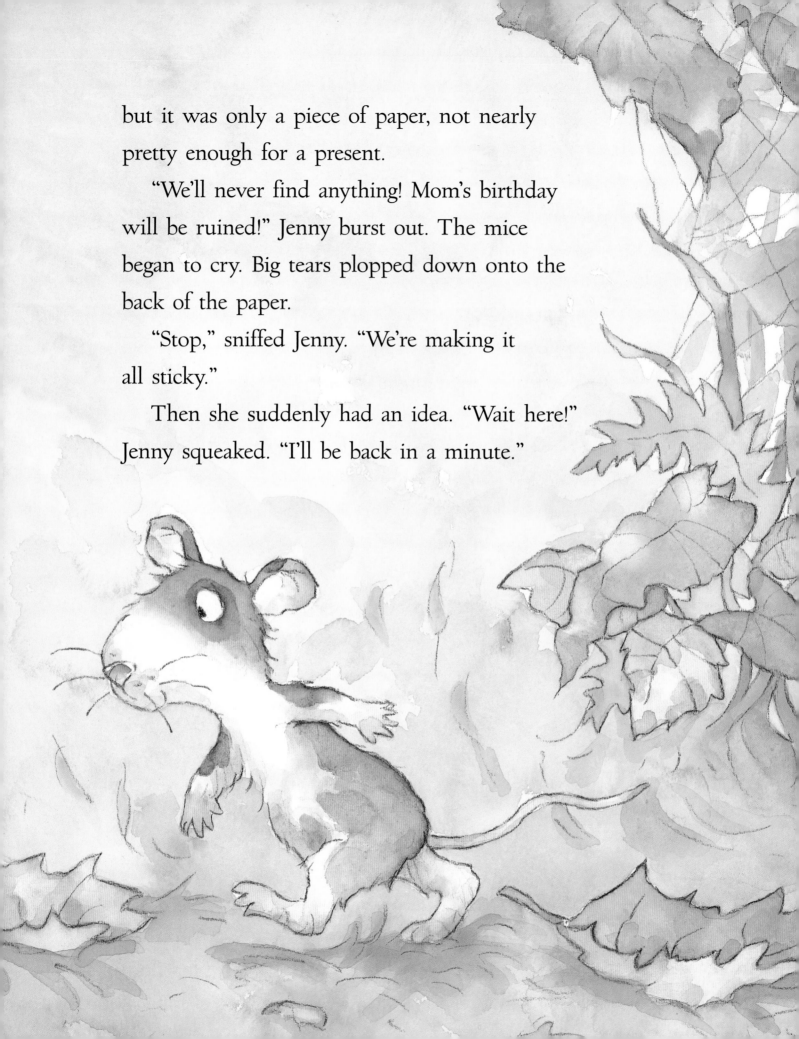

but it was only a piece of paper, not nearly
pretty enough for a present.

"We'll never find anything! Mom's birthday
will be ruined!" Jenny burst out. The mice
began to cry. Big tears plopped down onto the
back of the paper.

"Stop," sniffed Jenny. "We're making it
all sticky."

Then she suddenly had an idea. "Wait here!"
Jenny squeaked. "I'll be back in a minute."

Jenny raced off to find Vole, Bluejay, and Rabbit. They were happy to share a little bit of the things they had found that morning, and soon Jenny's arms were full as she ran back to her brothers and sister. They squeaked with excitement as Jenny told them her plan.

Soon they were all busy, shredding and sticking, until
at last the present was ready. The little mice ran home.

"Wake up, Mom! Happy birthday!" they giggled. "We've got a present just for you!"

Mother Mouse looked at the picture her children had made. It was red with strawberry, blue with feathers, and sprinkled golden with flower pollen.

"It's beautiful," she smiled, and hugged her mice close. "Thank you, everyone. It's the best birthday present ever."

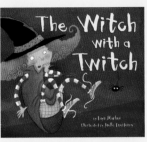

The Witch with a Twitch
by Layn Marlow
Illustrated by Joelle Dreidemy
ISBN-13: 978-1-58925-400-8
ISBN-10: 1-58925-400-7

Norman's Ark
by Michael Foreman
ISBN-13: 978-1-58925-401-5
ISBN-10: 1-58925-401-5

Clumsy Crab
by Ruth Galloway
ISBN-13: 978-1-58925-402-2
ISBN-10: 1-58925-402-3

Dinosaurs Galore!
by Giles Andreae
Illustrated by David Wojtowycz
ISBN-13: 978-1-58925-399-5
ISBN-10: 1-58925-399-X

Explore the world of tiger tales!

More fun-filled and exciting stories await you!
Look for these titles and more
at your local library or bookstore.
And have fun reading!

tiger tales
202 Old Ridgefield Road, Wilton, CT 06897

The Crunching Munching Caterpillar
by Sheridan Cain
Illustrated by Jack Tickle
ISBN-13: 978-1-58925-403-9
ISBN-10: 1-58925-403-1

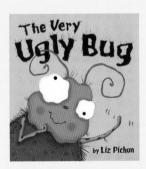

The Very Ugly Bug
by Liz Pichon
ISBN-13: 978-1-58925-404-6
ISBN-10: 1-58925-404-X

Good Night, Sleep Tight!
by Claire Freedman
Illustrated by Rory Tyger
ISBN-13: 978-1-58925-405-3
ISBN-10: 1-58925-405-8

Hound Dog
by David Bedford
Illustrated by Melanie Williamson
ISBN-13: 978-1-58925-397-1
ISBN-10: 1-58925-397-3